AND THE
DINO ATTACK

DEAR READER,

I've always wanted to be a superhero. I think that's what drew me to writing Marv. You can find countless pictures of me as a child dressed up in superhero costumes. I think that's pretty common right now, but what you have to understand is that when I grew up, I didn't have Marvel superhero movies coming out every other month—I had to make do with comics and cartoons.

One of those cartoons was called *Static Shock*. Its superhero was Static, a young black kid with electric powers who spouted cheesy one-liners as he zapped bad guys. Watching that show was the first time I had ever seen a young black boy be the hero of anything I'd ever watched or read. There was a reverence in the way that me and my friends watched and talked about *Static Shock*. We didn't have the language at that age to talk about representation and its importance, but deep down I know we all felt the same thing.

Static is a superhero, and he looks like us and that's really cool. He's one of us.

Quite a few years have passed since I was a kid watching *Static Shock*, and unfortunately, we don't have that many more prominent black superheroes. I cannot click my fingers and change this—after all, I am *not* a superhero. However, I feel that, by writing Marv and detailing his adventures, the laughs, and the struggles, I might give kids today the feeling I had all those years ago when I watched *Static Shock*.

Marv is a superhero, and he looks like us and that's really cool. He's one of us.

I hope you enjoy the book as much as I enjoyed writing it.

Alex

That's me!

OXFORD
UNIVERSITY PRESS

Great Clarendon Street, Oxford OX2 6DP

Oxford University Press is a department of the University of Oxford.
It furthers the University's objective of excellence in research, scholarship,
and education by publishing worldwide. Oxford is a registered trade mark
of Oxford University Press in the UK and in certain other countries

Database right Oxford University Press (maker)

First published in 2022

British Library Cataloguing in Publication Data

Data available

ISBN: 978-0-19-278044-7

3 5 7 9 10 8 6 4 2

Printed and bound by CPI Group (UK) Ltd, Croydon, CR0 4YY

Paper used in the production of this book is a natural,
recyclable product made from wood grown in sustainable forests.
The manufacturing process conforms to the environmental
regulations of the country of origin.

MARV
AND THE
DINO ATTACK

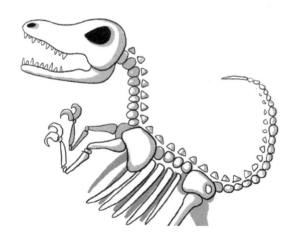

OXFORD
UNIVERSITY PRESS

CHAPTER 1

Marvin flicked through the dinosaur book on his lap. The pages were well worn, the new-book smell was long gone, but still, he always came back to it. For so long it had been the best way for him to see what dinosaurs had looked like, but that was all about to change because today he was going to the Natural History Museum with school. Marvin loved school trips, and he wasn't the only one. The school coach was filled with excited chatter. Their teacher had long ago given up on getting the class to be quiet.

'If you could be a dinosaur, any dinosaur, which one would you be?' Joe said from the seat next to Marvin.

'A pterodactyl, I think. I know it's not technically a dinosaur, but I'd love to be able to fly! To be whooshing through the clouds.' Marvin spread out his arms and flapped like a bird. 'What about you?'

'I'd be a velociraptor! They can run so fast, they might as well be flying.' Joe moved his legs back and forth quickly, pretending to run. 'But . . .'

'But what?' Marvin leant forward.

'We're missing the biggest and meanest one of all,' Joe whispered.

'A T-Rex!' Marvin shouted.

Joe roared in appreciation and raised his arms over his head.

Marvin burst out laughing.

'Being a T-Rex would be cool I guess. But what if you turned into a T-Rex and then tried to eat me?!' Marvin said.

'Yeah, good point. I definitely wouldn't want to be a T-Rex if it meant eating you for a tasty snack,' Joe replied with a grin.

High-pitched beeping filled the air. Marvin jolted upright in his seat.

'What's that sound?'

'Nothing.' Marvin shuffled uncomfortably, pushing his backpack further underneath his seat. It wasn't nothing. It was Pixel, Marvin's robot sidekick. Marvin took his super-suit and Pixel everywhere with him. 'Just in case', as his grandad would say. You

never know when a superhero would
be needed, so Marvin stayed ready. He
would have loved to tell Joe all about his
secret superhero identity and his super
sidekick, but his grandad had warned
him to keep his identity a secret.

Marvin wasn't surprised that Pixel was beeping; just like him, she was also excited about the school trip. Pixel had kept him up all night talking about it.

'Weird, I thought I definitely heard something.' Joe frowned.

'Erm . . . maybe someone on the coach has an alarm clock or something,' Marvin said. 'I'm thirsty so I'm just going to go pick up my water bottle.'

'Pixel, you have to be quiet.' Marvin leant down underneath his chair and whispered into his backpack, facing away from Joe.

Pixel popped her head out of the backpack. 'Apologies! My increased excitement levels appear to have compromised my beeping function again,' she whispered. Pixel had a round body and a small round head. She was silvery and smooth with long, ridged arms and huge round eyes. 'Are we nearly there yet?' she asked.

Marvin's eyebrows raised.

'If I tell you will you beep?'

'Maybe,' Pixel replied.

'We're slowing down!' Joe said excitedly, tugging Marvin back up. He looked out of the window, and there it was. The Natural History Museum!

It was an enormous building, tall and wide and made up of large slabs of grey brick. 'Wow,' Marvin gasped. This trip was going to be awesome.

When the coach pulled up outside the front, everyone cheered. Marvin glanced around at all those happy faces and found one person not smiling. The new girl, Eva. She was the only one in their whole class who was sat by herself. She had long black hair pulled up into a ponytail and sand-coloured skin. Instead of cheering, Eva was looking around anxiously, as though she wasn't sure whether to celebrate with the rest of the class.

Their teacher, Ms Davis, stood up at the front of the coach. She was a tall woman whose large afro brushed up against the ceiling.

'OK, quieten down now, please. As I'm sure you're all aware we have arrived at the museum.' The coach erupted into cheering again. Ms Davis shushed the class before speaking. 'Please remember that you are representing the school today, so be on your best behaviour. Now, don't forget your bags and you can follow me into the museum, in an orderly fashion.'

Marvin and Joe's eyes went wide as they entered the main hall. It was a large space with a huge domed ceiling

made of marble and a grand set of stairs
running up to the second floor.

An army of signs were laid out in front of them, each one giving directions to a different exhibition.

As well as the dinosaurs, there was an aquatic exhibition on, and Marvin could see off into another room where old submarines and scuba diving equipment were encased in glass displays.

'I-I-I don't know what to do first. It's all so cool,' Marvin said. He was so excited that he could barely get the words out.

'The aquatic exhibition looks good,' said Joe.

'Yes, but also they have like a million dinosaur fossils! We have to see them too.' Marvin pointed at another sign.

DINOSAURS

'Yeah, we have to see it all,' Joe said.

'And we will.' Marvin grinned. It was so great to have Joe as a best friend. He liked all the same things as Marvin. Things would be so much less fun without Joe around.

'Joe! Marvin! Come on!' Ms Davis called. Marvin glanced around and realized that in their excitement, they had wandered away from their class. Marvin and Joe hurried back to the group.

'All right children, we've arrived! Please remember to stay together; we don't want anyone getting lost. You'll be in pairs for our main activity today. Find a partner and complete the activity sheet, and we'll meet back up for lunch at twelve, in an hour and a half.'

Papers, clipboards, and pens were passed around the class. Marvin and Joe took theirs and then high-fived. They didn't even have to talk about it—of course they'd be working together. The dream team!

The rest of the class quickly paired up.

'Ah, looks as though we have an odd number today. Sorry, Eva, you'll be working with me today.'

Eva walked over to stand next to Ms Davis. Marvin was glad he didn't have to work with the teacher. That would have made everything boring. Marvin and Joe were going on an adventure today, and you can't go on an adventure with a teacher.

Eva stared at her feet, with her arms folded over her chest. Marvin took a step towards her. A hand gripped his shoulder and pulled him back.

It was Joe.

'Come on, Marvin! We can't waste a single second! We've got so much to see!' Joe yelled.

Marvin let Joe pull him away, and they rushed off towards the dinosaur exhibition.

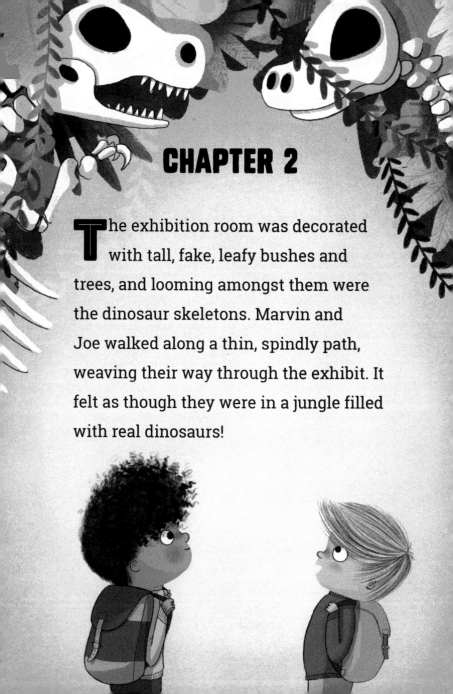

CHAPTER 2

The exhibition room was decorated with tall, fake, leafy bushes and trees, and looming amongst them were the dinosaur skeletons. Marvin and Joe walked along a thin, spindly path, weaving their way through the exhibit. It felt as though they were in a jungle filled with real dinosaurs!

Marvin and Joe didn't talk much, and they certainly didn't fill in their activity sheets. They just stared in awe. The occasional nod or whispered 'so cool' was all the communication that was needed. Marvin and Joe had been talking about this trip for weeks. It was an excellent opportunity to see and learn more about dinosaurs and Joe and Marvin were determined to make the most of it.

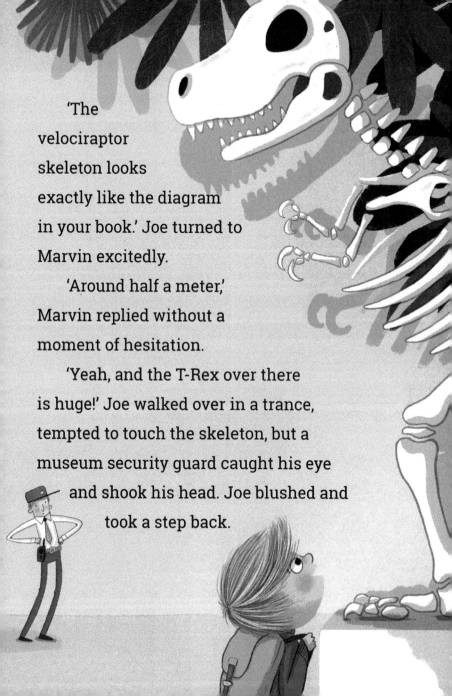

'The velociraptor skeleton looks exactly like the diagram in your book.' Joe turned to Marvin excitedly.

'Around half a meter,' Marvin replied without a moment of hesitation.

'Yeah, and the T-Rex over there is huge!' Joe walked over in a trance, tempted to touch the skeleton, but a museum security guard caught his eye and shook his head. Joe blushed and took a step back.

'The dinosaur skeletons look just like the ones in my book, but 3-D,' Marvin said, staring around in awe.

Just at that moment, Marvin felt a shiver up his back. He turned. A large shadow flashed across the back wall. It was only there for a second and then it was gone. Marvin froze. Something about this didn't feel right.

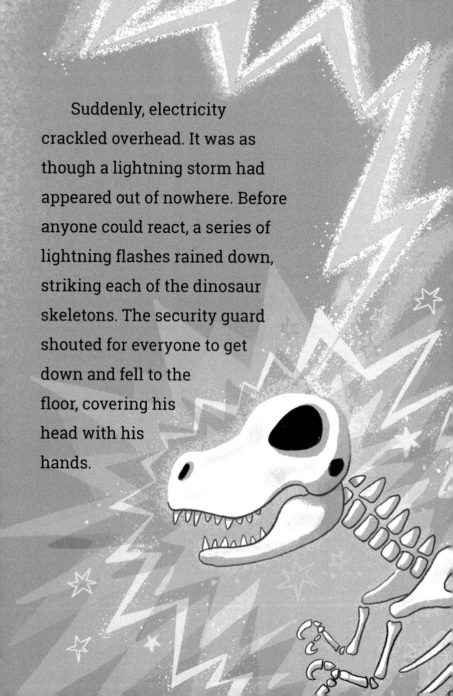

Suddenly, electricity crackled overhead. It was as though a lightning storm had appeared out of nowhere. Before anyone could react, a series of lightning flashes rained down, striking each of the dinosaur skeletons. The security guard shouted for everyone to get down and fell to the floor, covering his head with his hands.

The ground began to shake.

What was that?!

Something moved out of the corner of Marvin's eye. He turned around and studied the nearest dinosaur skeleton. It was small at first. A tiny twitch that was out of place. And then, before Marvin knew what was happening, the dinosaur skeletons were moving! They ripped themselves free from the plinths they were positioned on.

The dinosaurs stomped around the room, destroying what remained of the exhibit. They cracked the glass on the fossil cases and knocked all the fossils to the ground. The fake leaves and plants were crushed under their gigantic feet.

'Listen, children, we all just have to stay calm and not panic.' The security guard crawled over gingerly. A moment later, a small dinosaur walked past the guard, lightly brushing past his leg.

'Oh my gosh! A dinosaur attacked me! The dinosaurs are ALIVE!' the security guard yelped as he ran away.

The dinosaur skeletons lined up at the front of the room, near the door. Then they leant forward and bowed. Just then, a boy swaggered forward with his hands on his hips. He wore a black, leathery suit and had short spiky hair.

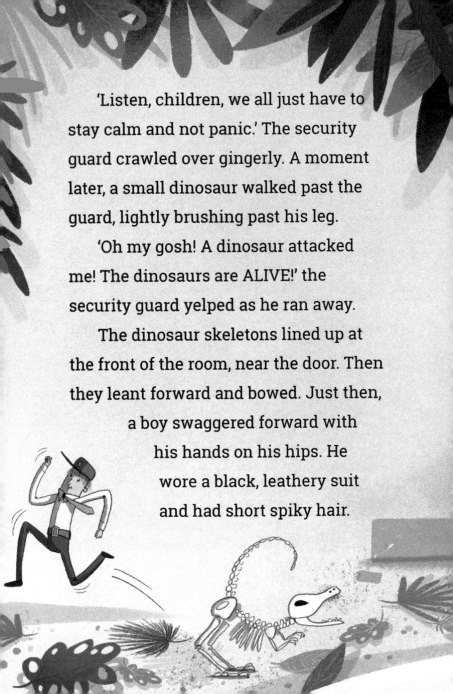

He walked from dinosaur to dinosaur, inspecting each one. When he touched them, a spark of electricity crackled over the place he had made contact with the skeletons. The electricity looked like the lightning that had struck the dinosaurs only moments before. Finally, the boy inspected the T-Rex. He smirked and then jumped up onto its back.

'You'll be my sidekick!' the boy yelled, then he turned to the rest of the room. 'I am Rex! If you know what's good for you, you'll stay out of my way!'

Rex marched the T-Rex out of the
door and all the rest of the dinosaur
skeletons followed after them.

'I think we need a hero.' Joe gulped
as he stumbled back.

'Yes, I think we do,' Marvin replied in his bravest voice. 'Stay here and try to hide. I'll go find our teacher.' That was what Marvin said, but in fact, he had no intention of finding their teacher.

Dinosaur skeletons were coming to life at the hands of a supervillain. And where there is a supervillain, there must also be a superhero. A superhero like Marv. So, Marvin dunked underneath a fossil display and ripped off his clothes, revealing his super-suit underneath. It was blue with a pulsing white 'M' over his chest. The suit could do anything, and it could give Marvin any power he desired. He just had to imagine it. The suit was powered by two things:

kindness and imagination. To everyone who saw him, he was no longer Marvin the boy, he was Marv the superhero!

Marv opened up his backpack.

'Supervillain detected! Supervillain detected!' Pixel chirped as she popped out.

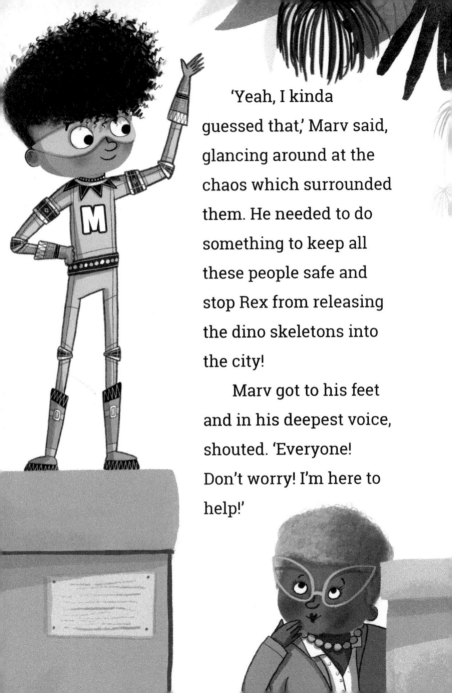

'Yeah, I kinda guessed that,' Marv said, glancing around at the chaos which surrounded them. He needed to do something to keep all these people safe and stop Rex from releasing the dino skeletons into the city!

Marv got to his feet and in his deepest voice, shouted. 'Everyone! Don't worry! I'm here to help!'

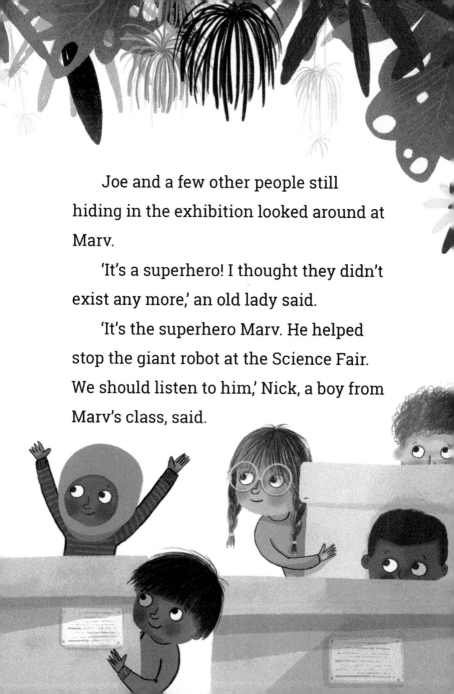

Joe and a few other people still hiding in the exhibition looked around at Marv.

'It's a superhero! I thought they didn't exist any more,' an old lady said.

'It's the superhero Marv. He helped stop the giant robot at the Science Fair. We should listen to him,' Nick, a boy from Marv's class, said.

'His name is Marv, sort of like the Marvin in our class.' Ayo, another child in Marv's class came forward.

'Our Marvin is quite a bit shorter than this Marv though.'

Marvin felt proud that people remembered who he was as a superhero, but he was also pretty sure that the suit didn't make him any taller.

'Have no fear! I'm going to find a way to stop Rex and put things right.' The problem was that Marv had no idea how to actually stop Rex. The super-villain and his T-Rex sidekick were nowhere to be seen.

'Marv!' A familiar voice called out.

Marv whipped around to find Joe, hiding underneath a bench. 'That super-villain is heading for the museum entrance. You can't let him escape with the dinosaurs!' Joe pointed at the doorway.

Marv just caught sight of a long, bony dino tail slinking through the door. Joe was right. If Rex managed to make it out of the museum with even one of the dinosaurs, then the mayhem wouldn't just be contained to the museum; it would be citywide. Marv had to stop him!

CHAPTER 3

Marv followed the trail of destruction left in Rex's wake to the aquatic exhibition. Water had been spilt all over the floor. The ancient-looking heavy diving equipment had been tossed aside. Rusty old submarines had been smashed into pieces. There were cracks in the floor where the dinosaurs had been stomping. Rex had definitely been here, and recently too. Marv followed the broken submarine parts and touched the 'M' on his suit. He would need some new powers if he was going to stand a chance against Rex and his army of dinosaurs. His suit began to buzz underneath its surface and the 'M' on his chest glowed.

Marv saw a triceratops skeleton walking around aimlessly up ahead. It looked lost and a bit confused, as though it didn't know what to do now that it had been brought back to life. Rex didn't seem to have total control over all the dino skeletons after all.

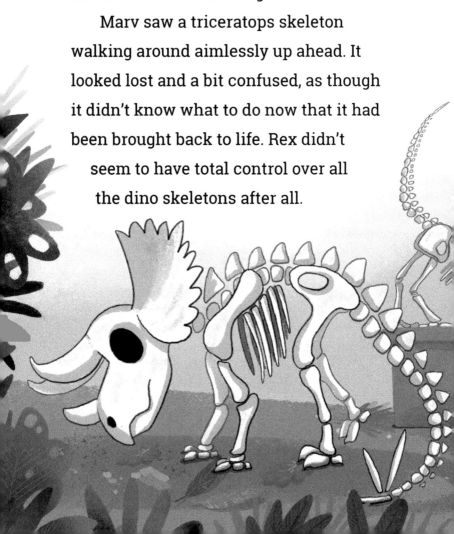

'I'm not scared because I'm a robot, and robots obviously never get scared, but I hope that we don't have to fight one of those,' Pixel said as they ran past the triceratops.

'Hopefully, we won't,' Marv said as they ran through the exhibit. 'Do you have any ideas on how we can stop Rex, Pixel?'

'Unfortunately, I was programmed to be a sidekick, not a superhero. My function is more supportive than directive,' Pixel replied. Marv stared back blankly. He didn't understand a word that had come out of Pixel's mouth. 'To be clear, as your grandad once said, "you're not too good with ideas, Pixel, you're more of an execution gal",' Pixel said, perfectly copying Grandad's voice.

'I didn't know that you could copy voices!' Marvin said.

'Voice copying has a five out of five rating on robotsidekicksuperpowers.com. It's an essential skill,' she said sternly.

'I'm sorry, I don't think I've been on that website before,' Marv replied.

Suddenly, with superhero reflexes,
Marv grabbed Pixel and leapt sideways.

The whooshing sound of two
enormous wings came from above.
Marv looked up. It was a pterodactyl. A
skeleton pterodactyl!

CAWWWWWWWWWW!

The pterodactyl circled around overhead, watching Marv and Pixel. Then it dived down—with Pixel in its sights! Underneath the museum lights, her silvery body was shining like a lighthouse.

'IT'S SUPER-SUIT TIME!' Marv yelled. 'Suit! Please activate catching net ability.' A small black box popped up out of the arm of his suit and a large net rocketed from it, wrapping tightly around the flying reptile in mid-dive.

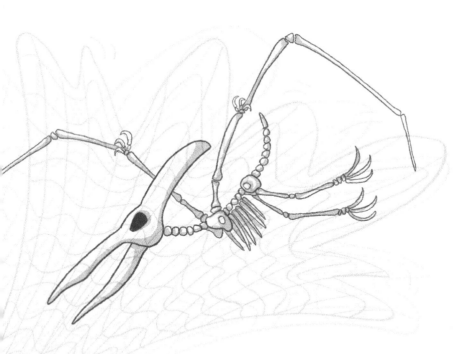

It roared as it came
crashing down to the ground with
a great thump. Marv flinched as it hit the
floor beside him.

The pterodactyl strained against the
net but couldn't break it.

'I'm sorry, Mr pterodactyl. We'll find a
way to turn you back into a fossil.'

Very carefully, Marv knelt down and reached out to gently stroke the captured reptile. It stopped struggling and seemed to calm down.

Pixel whizzed forward. A blue laser came out of her eyes and scanned the pterodactyl's body.

'That might be hard. I've analyzed the dinosaur, but there seems to be no scientific reason why this pterodactyl fossil has come to life,' Pixel said.

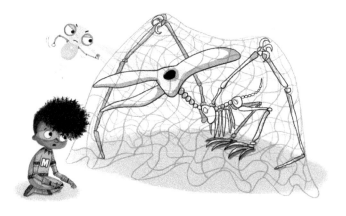

'What does that mean? What was in that electric bolt?' Marv replied.

Pixel buzzed around the room and then came back to Marv's side.

'I'm detecting high levels of supervillain powers all across the exhibit,' Pixel said.

'We're definitely dealing with a real supervillain here, and I suspect that stopping him will be the only way to turn these live skeletons back into fossils.' Marv swallowed.

'My superhero success tracker currently gives us a 99% chance of success,' Pixel said. 'We should have great chances to win here.'

'Whoa! You have a superhero success tracker?!' Marv leant forward.

'Yes,' Pixel said confidently. Then slowly, her head slumped. 'Actually, apologies, I lied. I don't have a tracker. There are no scientific reasons for me believing in us, but I still do. I have 99% confidence. I believe we will win because it's you and me.'

'You're a great sidekick, Pixel.' Marv nodded.

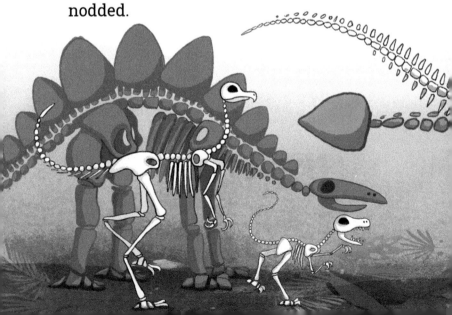

They took off again, following the
trail all the way to the end of the exhibit
through a doorway and into the back of
a very long line of dinosaur skeletons.
They were standing at the top of the
grand staircase that Marv had seen
when he had arrived at the museum that
morning. The way out of the museum
was just at the bottom of those stairs!

Rex was at the top of the stairs, perched on the back of his T-Rex. He was trying to force it to walk down the stairs, but it didn't seem too keen. He hadn't even noticed that Marv and Pixel were watching him.

'We're so close to the exit, you dumb beast! Keep going! I want a dinosaur sidekick. You're coming with me!' Rex snarled.

Marv gasped. A sidekick wasn't something you could steal. A sidekick was a friend, someone to accompany you on your journey and help you out when you needed it. What Rex was doing wasn't just selfish and wrong; it showed that Rex didn't really know anything

about what it meant to be a sidekick or what it meant to be a friend. The 'M' on Marv's chest glowed again and he felt a tingling sensation in his hands and feet.

'Hey! Rex!' Marv called out. Rex swivelled around to face him. 'These dinosaurs don't belong to you! You can't just take them!'

'I can take whatever I like! And you can't do anything to stop me!' Rex laughed and turned around. Marv looked past Rex to the exit. It was so close.

Marv had to find a way to get there first, but how could he when Rex and all his dinosaurs were in the way?

Marv had to come up with a plan, and fast!

CHAPTER 4

Marv glanced around, looking for something, anything, that might help block the exit to the museum. He remembered the pterodactyl, captured in the other room. That was it! Like a flash, the idea shot into Marv's head. He didn't know if it would work, but he had to try.

'You're coming with me, Pixel. Hold onto your butt.' Marv scooped up Pixel in his arms and took a deep breath. Pixel beeped, looked him in the eyes, and then nodded.

Marv took a couple of steps back before sprinting expertly past the queuing dinosaurs, towards the top of the staircase. Marv leapt over the staircase bannister. He hung in the air for a moment and then dropped straight down. His stomach backflipped as he fell. He really hoped this was going to work.

'Wings of a pterodactyl! Activate!'
Marv shouted. Two large, mechanical
wings sprouted out of Marv's suit. After
a couple of long and fluid flaps, Marv
was no longer falling. He soared through
the air, swooping left and right. The air

whooshed past his face. Marv couldn't help but grin. Being a superhero could be really fun sometimes. He landed at the bottom of the staircase, right in front of the museum exit.

It wasn't a moment too soon, because Rex had finally managed to force his T-Rex down the stairs and he too, was heading straight for the exit.

'Get outta my way!' Rex looked down from atop his dinosaur, sneering at Marv. 'Can't you see that I'm trying to leave?' Rex wobbled back and forth on the T-Rex. It was making jerky movements, as though it was unsure of where to go next. Rex forced it to the left, but Marv jumped in front of their path.

'I can't let you leave, Rex, you know that,' Marv said with a firm shake of the head. He spread his arms wide, doing his best to keep Rex from going past him.

'And who're you to think you can stop someone like me?!' Rex was hopping mad. He bounced up and down on the dinosaur. He got so mad that

lightning accidentally burst out from
the palms of his hands, striking the floor
with a thunderous sound. The T-Rex
reared up and dumped Rex onto the
floor. 'Whooooaaa!' Rex
shouted as he fell.

The T-Rex stomped away, leaving Rex all on his own. The rest of the dinosaur skeletons followed suit, stomping off in all different directions. While Rex was on the floor, Marv was struck by another idea. He spun around to face the exit.

'Super slime spitter! Activate!' Marv cried. Two small vents popped out of the forearms of his suit. Marv aimed his arms forward, and out of the vents came a thick, green sludge. It shot forward, splattering onto the exit doors, completely covering them in slime. In moments, the slime had dried and hardened.

Marv walked up to the doors and pushed as hard as he could. They didn't budge. There was no way anything could get through now. Marv had done it. He'd stopped Rex from taking the dinosaurs outside of the museum.

This wasn't finished, though.

Marv turned to see that Rex was dusting himself off.

'How dare you get in my way?!' Rex shook his head furiously.

'I'm a superhero, so of course I'm
going to stop you,' Marv said.

'It's not over yet!' Rex took a
threatening step in Marv's direction.
Marv pressed a finger against the 'M' on
his chest, then he turned around and
pushed Pixel back.

'Don't worry, Pixel, I'll keep you safe,'
Marv whispered, then turned back to face
the supervillain ahead. 'It's just you and
me, Rex.'

Rex leant back and gave a high-
pitched whistle.

'Really? Are you sure it's just you and
me?' A wide grin spread across Rex's face.

The ground began to rumble, just as it had done before.

Marv was confused for a moment, and then he understood. Dinosaurs. A whole group of them. They ran in on their hind legs, the claws on their feet clacking against the marble floor. Their teeth were long and sharp.

'If I can't have the T-Rex, these velociraptors will have to do.'

Marv took a step back. His stomach dropped.

Rex broke out into a mean laugh.

The velociraptor skeletons surrounded Marv and Pixel.

'It seems that the numbers are no longer in our favour,' Pixel said.

'Yep. Seems like it,' Marv replied.

CHAPTER 5

Marv stood, frozen to the spot, as the velociraptors closed in. What was Marv supposed to do? He could use the net again, but the net only worked on one dinosaur, not six. And even if he did catch them, they'd probably just chew their way out. Their teeth looked much stronger than the pterodactyl's. He needed something else, but he didn't know what that something else might be. The velociraptors were almost upon them.

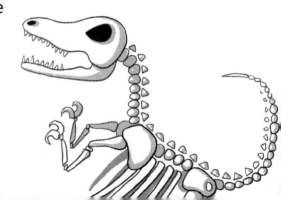

'Pixel! Hide! I'll deal with this.'

A velociraptor darted its head forward and snapped at Marv. It was quick—so quick that the entire move took less than a second. To Marv though, it felt as though the velociraptor was moving in slow motion. Marv dodged back. His reactions were a hundred times quicker than they were without the suit.

Marv could feel the suit making his reflexes more sensitive and making him faster than he had ever been before.

Marv felt a surge of power and he sprang into the air, somersaulting over the circle of velociraptors, taking Pixel with him. He could hear Rex's cackle as he ran.

The velociraptors sprinted after Marv, snapping at his heels. They could get close, but they couldn't catch him. The super speed in Marv's legs kept him safe. But he couldn't run for ever.

Marv suddenly had a flash of inspiration, but would it work? He didn't know, but still, he had to try and trust in the power of his suit.

Marv pressed the 'M' on his suit and muttered an order. Then he stopped and leapt around, turning to face the velociraptors head-on.

'Freeze!' Marv shouted, pointing directly at one of the beasts. Out of Marv's outstretched finger came a blue bolt. It hit the velociraptor, but it didn't do anything. The dinosaur was still running right at Marv. He closed his eyes. This was it—the suit had failed him!

Marv opened his eyes. A velociraptor stood over him, but it wasn't moving. He reached out and touched it. The velociraptor had been frozen in action. It had been turned back into a normal skeleton.

The suit had come through for Marv after all.

Marv glanced beyond the frozen dinosaur to the rest of the velociraptors. They stood still, not daring to come any closer.

Marv lifted his hand and began to point.

'Freeze! Freeze! Freeze! Freeze! Freeze!' Marv yelled, pointing at each of the velociraptors. Five blasts shot out of his fingertip.

Direct hits.

A freezing dryness spread from

where they had been hit to the rest of their bodies. In mere moments, all the velociraptors were still. They had been frozen solid. Marv let out a breath he had been holding for a while, then smiled. He had done it!

Now for Rex!

His super speed flooded down into his legs, turbocharging them again.

To Marv's surprise, Rex had some more supervillain tricks up his sleeve. His hands had been transformed into thick dinosaur claws and he was using them to scamper up a wall next to the museum exit. Not too far above him was an open window. Rex had obviously abandoned the idea of a dinosaur sidekick and was now trying to escape!

Marv crouched down and felt super strength build up in his legs, ready to strike.

'Dinosaur, please cease your actions. It would be very inconvenient if you were to eat me. I wouldn't be able to carry out my sidekick duties.' Marv heard Pixel's voice from behind.

Marv turned around. The T-Rex was lumbering straight at Pixel. Her arms flailed in the air as she backed away, afraid.

Rex had almost reached the window.

'Dinosaur, please rethink your actions! You are a carnivore, and I am a mere robot. I was not built to be tasty,' Pixel continued.

Marv knew what he must do.

'Freeze!'

The T-Rex roared as the bolt from Marv's finger froze it on the spot. Now he was just a skeleton once more.

Marv turned to see Rex leap towards the open window.

'You saved me instead of catching the supervillain. Are you sure that was the correct choice of action?' Pixel cried, speeding over to Marv's side.

'I think superheroes should save people . . . and robots.' Marv rubbed the top of Pixel's head affectionately and she beeped loudly.

'That sounds like the kind of superhero I want to be a sidekick for.'

CHAPTER 6

Marv ran over to the window and
watched as Rex climbed down the
outside of the museum. There was no
way Marv could follow him now—there
were still dinosaurs to freeze.

'Smell you later, loser!' Rex called out
as he reached the pavement.

'That's strange,' Pixel said.

'What is?' Marv replied.

'Is it common for humans who have lost badly and had to run away, to call the person who beat them a "loser"?' Pixel asked.

Marv burst into laughter as Rex disappeared around the corner and out into the city.

Marv and Pixel glanced around the messy museum. A whole host of dinosaurs looked back at them.

'Well, it's time to clean up this museum. There are dinosaurs that need to be frozen! Come on, Pixel.' Marv broke into a run. Super speed kicked in again. Every time Marv ran into a dinosaur, he'd point at it and yell, 'freeze!'

Pixel followed after him, fixing broken exhibits and tidying away the mess left by the rampaging beasts.

Once Marv finished freezing the last
dinosaur, he stumbled upon
Eva, hiding under a table.

'Is it over?' she
whispered.

'Hey Ev—' Marv
stopped, realizing
that it would be a little
suspicious if a superhero
Eva had never spoken to,
knew her name. 'Ahem—
hello, my name is Marv, and I'm
a superhero. You don't need to fear. The
dinosaurs are just normal skeletons
again,' Marv said, trying to make his
voice a bit deeper to disguise it.

'Thank you.' Eva crawled out into the open. 'Whoa!' she cried as Pixel hovered over to where they were.

'That's my sidekick, Pixel,' Marv said.

'No way!' Eva crouched down and leant closer to Pixel, with an excited grin on her face.

'One of my aunts is very into robotics so I know a bit about robots. This is super high-tech!'

'Wait, you like robots?!'

'Of course, they're the coolest,' Eva said, standing up.

'And what about dinosaurs?' Marv asked.

'Pretty cool except for when they're trying to eat you,' Eva laughed, and Marv laughed too.

Here was somebody who liked dinosaurs and robots just like Marv and Joe did. Marv wished he had spoken to Eva sooner.

Marv led Eva through the museum, searching for the rest of their class. The other museum-goers were emerging from their hiding places too, and they pointed at him, whispering as he walked past. 'Look! It's the superhero Marv!'

Marv and Eva made their way to the dinosaur exhibit where the adventure had first begun.

'It's safe to come out now,' Marv called.

Ms Davis peeped her head around a large fossil. 'No more moving dinosaur skeletons?' she asked, nervously.

'No more moving dinosaur skeletons,' Marv replied.

'All right, children, come on out!' Marv's class emerged from their hiding places looking at Marv in amazement. 'Thank you, Marv,' Ms Davis said. 'It looks as though you've saved the day once again.'

'Yeah, thanks, Marv,' said Ayo.

'Super Marv to the rescue!' Nick yelled.

'Marv, you're awesome!' Yasmin, another child in his class, called out.

'Three cheers for Marv!' the whole class shouted.

Marv couldn't help but smile. It felt so good to have his hard work appreciated and to be seen as a hero, but he knew he couldn't stay here for ever.

'Thank you, but I have to go now. My work here is done!'

Marv ran away from his cheering class with a grin on his face. Pixel followed.

'Laser blast, activate!' Marv said as he reached the exit. A laser shot out of his outstretched finger and smashed into the hard slime Marv had put over the door. It cracked and crumbled to the floor. Marv whizzed back around to his backpack and neatly changed into his normal clothes, without anyone noticing.

'Superhero mission accomplished,'
Pixel said happily.

'Yeah, somehow we managed to save
the day. That's the power of teamwork.'
Marvin smiled. He opened his backpack,
waiting for Pixel to jump inside, but she
just hovered in place, staring at him.
'Pixel, are you waiting for something?'

'It seems that you have forgotten
our protocol for when we finish
superheroing.' Pixel cocked her head
sideways.

'What's that?' Marvin said.

'If I recall correctly, you humans refer
to it as a "high five".'

'Oh yeah, I forgot.' Marvin reached out to Pixel, and she slapped her hand into his.

Marvin grinned as he watched Pixel jump into his backpack. She really was the best sidekick around.

CHAPTER 7

With his super-suit hidden under his normal clothes, and Pixel safely back in his backpack, Marvin went off to find his class.

Marvin was heading back to his class when he bumped into two women with long grey hair, thick glasses, and matching rainbow-coloured T-shirts.

'Oh, sorry for bumping into you. We're the museum curators. We heard there was a disturbance, so we came to make sure that nothing was damaged and that everyone is safe.'

'A little late for that. We had to rely on a superhero to save the day,' one man said as he walked by, shaking his cane at the curators.

'It seems there has been a sharp increase in the number of super-villains on the loose. We'll have to be more careful. And thank goodness for superheroes,' one of the curators said. The other one took her glasses off and leant in close to inspect one of the dinosaur skeletons Marv had frozen. She tapped at it with her finger.

'On the plus side, we do have some impressive new poses for our dinosaur skeletons, very action packed,' she said.

The curators were right, there did seem to be an increase in the number of supervillains on the loose. Luckily, there was a new superhero in town too!

Just then, Marvin's teacher rushed over.

'Marvin! I'm so glad that you're safe. Please remember to stay close to your classmates. It was very irresponsible for you to go wandering off with all those dinosaurs on the loose.'

'Sorry,' Marvin replied.

If only she knew . . .

'Marvin!' Joe rushed over and threw his arms around his best friend. 'What happened? Where did you go?'

'I went to find help but then I got separated from you guys and had to hide.' Marvin scratched at his head and chuckled.

'We're alright because Marvin—I mean, Marv, defeated the supervillain and saved the day. Did you see him when you were out in the museum?' Joe said with a strange, knowing smile on his face. Marvin's heart beat faster. Did Joe say Marvin by accident, or was it on purpose? Did Joe know his secret identity?!

'Nope. I must have just missed him.'
Marvin shrugged, trying his best to look
as though he didn't care.

'Right, children. Let's head to the
canteen for lunch. I'm sure you're
starving after all that excitement.'

Marvin's teacher clapped her hands together and they followed her into the canteen.

'Marvin, let's sit together! We've missed so much time because of that supervillain, so we need to really come up with a strategy, so we can see everything we need to see.'

'Yeah, that sounds good. Just give me one second.' Marvin left Joe at one of the dining tables and went off in search of someone. He didn't have to look for long.

Eva was sat by herself, just about to tuck into her lunch.

'Hey,' Marvin tapped her on the shoulder.

'Hey,' Eva replied.

'Would you like to hang out with Joe and me this afternoon?' Marvin said.

'Are you sure?' Eva perked up in her seat.

'Yeah, we could really use a third person in our group. We're trying to see as much of the museum as we can with the time we have left so we need to come up with a plan. Three brains are better than two.' Marvin reached out his hand. 'Teammates?'

'Teammates!' Eva grasped his hand and shook it hard.

Marvin grinned—he was looking forward to having a new friend.

ABOUT THE AUTHOR

ALEX FALASE-KOYA

Alex is a London native. He has been both reading and writing since he was a teenager and was a winner of Spread the Word's 2019 London Writers Awards for YA and Children's. He now lives in Walthamstow with his girlfriend and two cats.

ABOUT THE ILLUSTRATOR

PAULA BOWLES

Paula grew up in Hertfordshire, and has always loved drawing, reading, and using her imagination, so she studied illustration at Falmouth College of Arts and became an illustrator. She now lives in Bristol, and has worked as an illustrator for over ten years, and has had books published with Nosy Crow and Simon & Schuster.

MARV

Marvin's life changed when he found an old superhero suit and became MARV. The suit has been passed down through Marvin's family and was last worn by his grandad. It's powered by the kindness and imagination of the wearer, and doesn't work for just anybody.

COURAGE	7
FRIENDSHIP	9
KINDNESS	9
POWERS	10
AGILITY	7
COMBAT SKILLS	6

PIXEL

PIXEL is Marv's brave superhero sidekick. Her quick thinking and unwavering loyalty make her the perfect crime-fighting companion.

COURAGE	6
FRIENDSHIP	10
KINDNESS	9
POWERS	5
AGILITY	7
COMBAT SKILLS	5

REX

REX has an unusual set of powers linked to animals. He can communicate with animals and bring dinosaur skeletons to life. He'd love to have an army of deadly creatures that obey his every command.

COURAGE	5
FRIENDSHIP	4
KINDNESS	4
POWERS	7
AGILITY	7
COMBAT SKILLS	7

SUIT UP. STEP UP.
IT'S TIME TO BECOME A **HERO!**

MARV

AND THE
MEGA
ROBOT

WRITTEN BY
ALEX FALASE-KOYA

PICTURES BY
PAULA BOWLES

'THE SUPER-SUIT IS POWERED BY TWO THINGS: KINDNESS AND IMAGINATION. LUCKILY YOU, MARVIN, HAVE TONS OF BOTH!'

Marvin loves reading about superheroes and now he's about to become one for real.

Grandad is passing his superhero suit and robot sidekick, Pixel, on to Marvin. It's been a long time since the world needed a superhero but now, with a mega robot and a supervillain on the loose, that time has come.

To defeat his enemies and protect his friends, Marvin must learn to trust the superhero within. Only then will Marvin become MARV – unstoppable, invincible, and **totally marvellous!**

LOVE MARV?
WHY NOT TRY THESE TOO...?